A Slice of the Blarney

by

Kitty Burns

SAMUEL FRENCH

FOUNDED 1830

NEW YORK HOLLYWOOD LONDON TORONTO

SAMUELFRENCH.COM

IMPORTANT BILLING AND CREDIT REQUIREMENTS

All producers of *A SLICE OF THE BLARNEY must* give credit to the Author of the Play in all programs distributed in connection with performances of the Play, and in all instances in which the title of the Play appears for the purposes of advertising, publicizing or otherwise exploiting the Play and/or a production. The name of the Author *must* appear on a separate line on which no other name appears, immediately following the title and *must* appear in size of type not less than fifty percent of the size of the title type.

CHARACTERS

SHANNON O'LEARY. . . . . 60-65 – Crotchety, old man

DOUGLAS O'LEARY . . . . 40's-50's – Loud mouth, Shannon's brother

KATIE O'LEARY . . . . 20's – Sweet, caring,
Shannon's youngest daughter

ARLENE O'LEARY. . . . . 50's – Headstrong, Shannon's ex-wife

SHARON O'LEARY . . . . 30's – Shannon's daughter. Gypsy-like, fun.
Thinks she's psychic.

PATRICK O'LEARY . . . . 20's – Chip on his shoulder, Shannon's Son

COLLEEN SULLIVAN . . . . . . .30's – Pleasant, especially toward Shannon.
Shannon's maid.

TIME

Present

SETTING

Shannon O'Leary's house in a town right outside of Manhattan.

The World Premiere
of an Original Comedy
in Two Acts

"A $lice of the Ⓑlarney"
by Kitty Burns

Directed by Lewis Hauser

Dramatis Personae
(in order of appearance)

Shannon O'Leary	....	*Tim Holtwick*
Katie O'Leary	....	*Catherine Michaels*
Colleen Sullivan	....	*Stephanie Carr*
Douglas O'Leary	....	*Robert Malcheski*
Arlene O'Leary	....	*Alice Lunsford*
Patrick O'Leary	....	*Seth Gillum*
		or Trevor Wilde
Sharon O'Leary	....	*Jacee Jule*
Dr. Goldberg	....	*Lewis Hauser*

The setting is Shannon O'Leary's house, in a town right outside of
Manhattan.
It is Christmastime, present day.

There will be a 15-minute intermission

between the first and second acts

Set and lighting design and booth operation by Kevin Patrick Wright

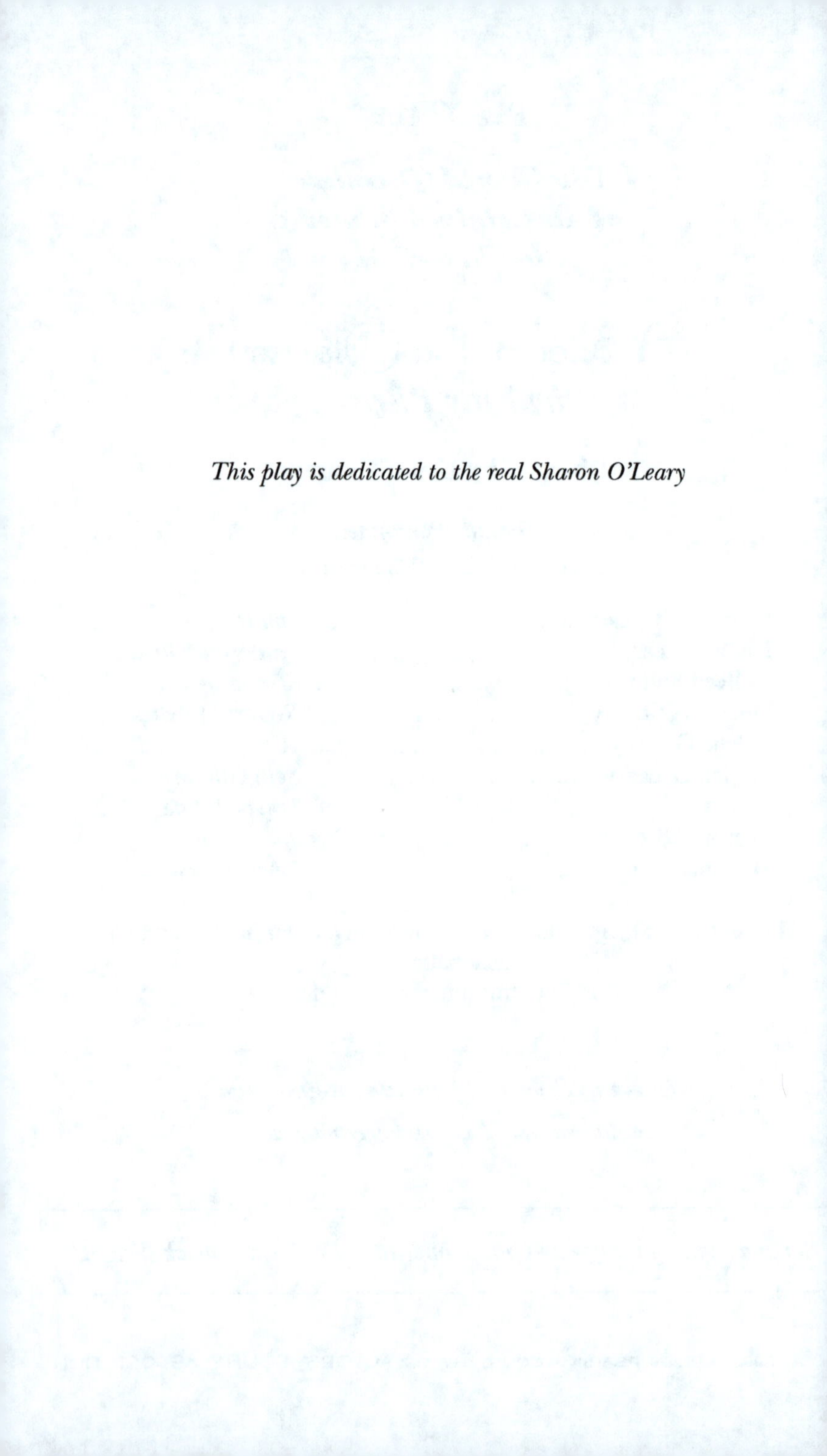

This play is dedicated to the real Sharon O'Leary

ACT ONE

(The living room is decorated for Christmas, with a tree in the upstage right corner of the room and a banner saying, "Peace on Earth" on the wall above the rifle. A few other Christmas decorations are throughout the room [not overdone].)

(SHANNON *is in his bed reading.* **DOUGLAS** *is walking out of Shannon's room into the living room where* **KATIE** *is sitting on the couch.)*

SHANNON. *(Yelling to* **DOUGLAS** *as he leaves the bedroom)* I'll be out livin' all of you just to drive you crazy!

DOUGLAS. He's pushing me too far. *(Goes over to wet bar and fixes himself a drink)* I can't take this much longer.

KATIE. *(Sadly)* You won't have to take this much longer. The doctor said it's just a matter of time.

DOUGLAS. Just a matter of time, my ass. He's probably helping Shannon drag this out on purpose. He still has one more boy to put through college. All I know is, I for one have spent too much time putting up with that bastard in there.

KATIE. He means well.

DOUGLAS. Means well? All he does is threaten to cut me out of his Will because he hates the way I'm running his damned business.

KATIE. You know he'd never do that.

DOUGLAS. I don't know what he'd do.

KATIE. You're his brother. No matter how much he complains, he loves you. He'd never admit it, but he thinks the world of you.

DOUGLAS. Yeah. That's why he keeps telling everyone I'm the black sheep of the family because I was born in the States so I'm not a real Irishman.

KATIE. You know that's just his way of bating you. He's been doing it since you were kids.

DOUGLAS. Well, I'm sick of it.

KATIE. Where would you two be without your daily battles?

DOUGLAS. I can't wait to find out. I just wish he'd hurry up and put us all out of our misery.

KATIE. You shouldn't talk that way. I hope to God that you two make peace with each other before it's too late.

DOUGLAS. Katie, you're a dear, sweet girl, but as God is my witness, I'll never understand how you can live here and take care of that man!

KATIE. *That man* is my father. I know he's not perfect, but he's always been good to me, and as long as he's alive, I'll be good to him.

DOUGLAS. I've never been able to figure you out. Either you're as sweet as you seem and you really do love the old fart, or you're a martyr who has sentenced herself to Hell on earth, or you're a conniving, back-stabbing suck-up who's just after his money – like the rest of us.

KATIE. How dare you! *(Enters Shannon's room.)* I can't stand having them here.

SHANNON. I know, Katie, me darlin', but surely you won't be putting up with them much longer.

KATIE. Dinner will be ready soon. Why don't you come out and sit at the table tonight. I hate to see you spend all day and all night in your room by yourself.

SHANNON. I haven't been by meself, and I have you to thank for that. You've come in and kept me company three times today. You're an angel from heaven, Katie, me darlin'.

KATIE. Then do me a favor and join us at the table for dinner tonight.

SHANNON. I'll think about it.

KATIE. Come on, Dad. The whole family will be here. It won't be the same without you.

SHANNON. All right. If it means that much to you, I'll be there.

(The doorbell rings.)

DOUGLAS. I'll get it. *(Opens the door)* Oh, it's you.

ARLENE. *(Enters and kisses **DOUGLAS** on the cheek.)* Merry Christmas to you too, Douglas.

DOUGLAS. You look well.

ARLENE. Yes, so do you.

SHANNON. You know, that's the worst part about dying. All the ghosts from your past come back to haunt you. Couldn't she have waited till I died to come and harass me? Now I know what they mean when they say, "May you be in heaven a half hour before the devil knows you're dead."

KATIE. I'll try to keep her away from you as much as I can.

SHANNON. God bless you, darlin'.

*(**KATIE** enters the living room.)*

KATIE. Mother.

ARLENE. Katie, you look wonderful.

KATIE. Thank you, Mother. So do you. *(Hugs **ARLENE**)*

ARLENE. What a hideous trip I had. First class was oversold, so I had to sit in coach. And if they think just reimbursing me for the difference between a first class ticket and a coach ticket is going to pacify me, they're sadly mistaken. They're also going to pay me back the $5.00 I spent to watch that stupid movie, and the $32.00 it cost me to drink my way across the country. It was the only way I could survive sitting next to that horrible screaming baby! And don't even get me started on the food!

KATIE. Well, other than that, Mrs. Lincoln, how was the play?

ARLENE. Kathryn Margaret, you know how I hate being put out.

KATIE. All too well.

ARLENE. Then have a little sympathy. I don't think it's asking too much to be treated with the respect I deserve.

KATIE. Of course not, Mother.

> (**ARLENE** *looks around the room and focuses on the Christmas tree.*)

ARLENE. *(Insincerely)* Nice tree.

KATIE. Thanks. Colleen and I did it.

ARLENE. Ah, so now it's down to two? I remember when we all did it together as a family. But, that was a long time ago.

DOUGLAS. So, Arlene, how long are you staying?

ARLENE. If you mean when will I be leaving, my plans are indefinite. So, how's business? Still prosperous I hope.

DOUGLAS. Don't worry, Arlene. Business is better than ever now that I'm running things. In fact, your million dollars in stocks is now worth double, thanks to me.

ARLENE. Well, I guess this trip will be worth the trouble after all. *(Shouts to the kitchen)* Colleen!

COLLEEN. *(Enters from kitchen)* Mrs. O'Leary, welcome back.

ARLENE. Yes. There's a man in a taxicab out in front waiting to be paid. While you're at it, bring in my bags.

COLLEEN. *(Under her breath)* Like I said, welcome back. *(Exits to the kitchen, then returns and goes out the front door)*

ARLENE. I'm starving. The food on that airplane wasn't fit for a dog.

KATIE. I'll make you a small sandwich.

ARLENE. A sandwich? How quaint.

KATIE. Dinner will be ready shortly, so you don't want to eat anything too heavy. By the way, Mother, in case you're interested, Dad is not doing well.

ARLENE. Oh yes, that's right. I almost forgot. How is my dear ex-husband?

DOUGLAS. Slipping further away day by day.

ARLENE. He always has been a procrastinator.

KATIE. Your compassion is overwhelming.

ARLENE. I have no compassion for the man.

KATIE. The man is dying.

ARLENE. The man is loitering.

(COLLEEN *enters with two bags of luggage and puts them inside by the front door. Then she goes out and brings in two more, then two more.*)

DOUGLAS. Are you moving back?

ARLENE. That'll be the day! This trip is going to be as short as possible, (*Looks towards Shannon's room*) God-willing.

KATIE. I'll go get you something to eat.

ARLENE. You'll do no such thing. Why do you think your father has a maid? (*pointing to* COLLEEN)

KATIE. You're a maid? You didn't tell me that!

COLLEEN. We've been keeping it from you.

ARLENE. It didn't take long for you two to remind me why I don't miss this madhouse. Tell me, Colleen. Do you and my ex-husband still play chess everyday?

COLLEEN. No. He stopped playing with me ever since I beat him two games in a row. Katie's his chess partner now.

ARLENE. That's too bad.

COLLEEN. It's okay. I still read James Joyce to him every night after his massage.

ARLENE. I'll bet you do.

COLLEEN. (*Coldly*) What would you like to eat, Mrs. O'Leary?

ARLENE. Anything is fine, as long as it is not surrounded by two pieces of bread.

DOUGLAS. Why don't you go say hello to the old man?

ARLENE. I suppose I should.

KATIE. Maybe you should have something to eat first, Mother.

ARLENE. No, let me get this over with. (*Exits to Shannon's room.*)

SHANNON. Well, Lord have mercy! Look who's here. Am I dreaming?

ARLENE. No, Shannon, you're not dreaming.

SHANNON. Damn!

(ARLENE *kisses Shannon on the forehead.*)

ARLENE. You look...*(Pause)*

SHANNON. Like poop?

ARLENE. Shannon, must you be so vulgar?

SHANNON. I only talk this way for you.

ARLENE. Is that supposed to make me feel special?

SHANNON. Unique.

ARLENE. I know I'm unique. I don't need you to tell me that. So what does the doctor say?

SHANNON. You'll be rid of me anytime now.

ARLENE. He's been saying that for months.

SHANNON. Then why did you suddenly believe him and come to visit me?

ARLENE. I didn't want it to end like this.

SHANNON. Like what? With me dying? All right, Arlene, I'll be a gentleman. You go first.

ARLENE. I mean with us hating each other.

SHANNON. Hating each other? I don't hate you. Actually, I find you rather amusing.

ARLENE. I am not amusing, and I am not amused. I mean it, Shannon. I want the hostility between us to end. We're both adults. I think it's time we were able to forgive and forget.

SHANNON. So you can live long and prosper? Don't worry, Arlene. You're in my Will.

ARLENE. I don't care about that. I want us to part friends.

SHANNON. Part friends? Darlin', we're not breaking off a courtship. I'm dying!

ARLENE. *(Starts to cry.)* I did the best I could, honest I did. I tried to be a good wife. I just didn't like coming second to your business.

SHANNON. You knew my work came first when you married me.

ARLENE. I thought you would stop working so hard once you became a success.

SHANNON. And surely I would have if I had listened to you, but praise be to God that I didn't. You stop working hard and you stop making money.

ARLENE. You didn't have to make this much money. We didn't need to become rich. We could have just been comfortable.

SHANNON. I can't believe you just said that. I had to keep making money to keep up with you're spending it. You can run up a credit card faster than a filly at the Sweepstakes.

ARLENE. You bought a few choice toys for yourself too, you know. You didn't need four cars and three sailboats.

SHANNON. Surely I did. They all gave me a way to get away.

ARLENE. But you never went anywhere. You were always working.

SHANNON. Aye, but I could have if I wanted to.

ARLENE. Shannon Joseph O'Leary, you're a very strange man.

SHANNON. That's what makes me so much fun.

ARLENE. I've got to go get something to eat. I'll see you at dinner.

SHANNON. *(Puts on his glasses to watch her walk out of the room)* All right, Sweet Cheeks, see you at dinner.

ARLENE. You start calling me that again and I'm going to get you right in the spizerinctom.

SHANNON. I'll stop calling you that when you tell me what the hell a spizerinctom is!

ARLENE. Look it up.

SHANNON. I've looked in every goddamn dictionary in the country. There's no such word.

ARLENE. If there was no such word, I couldn't be using it, now could I?

SHANNON. You just made it up to torment me, didn't you, Sweet Cheeks?

ARLENE. *(To herself:)* You got that right. *(To* **SHANNON:** *)* I'm warning you, Shannon. The next time you call me that, you're going to find out what a spizerinctom is – then you'll wish you didn't know.

SHANNON. Promises, promises.

(ARLENE *enters the living room.*)

ARLENE. Is Sharon going to be here tonight?

DOUGLAS. Yes, but she can't make it for dinner.

(COLLEEN *enters with a plate of cheese and crackers.* ARLENE *is fixing herself a drink.*)

COLLEEN. Will this do until dinner?

ARLENE. I suppose it will have to.

(*The doorbell rings.* COLLEEN *answers the door.* PATRICK *enters.*)

COLLEEN. Hi, Patrick.

PATRICK. Hi, Colleen. What's going on?

COLLEEN. Not much yet, but it's getting interesting. (*Enters the kitchen. Then begins setting the dining room table.*)

ARLENE. Patrick, dear, it's so good to see you. (*Hugs him*)

PATRICK. (*Sincerely*) It's good to see you too, Mother. I've really missed you.

ARLENE. I've missed you too, son.

DOUGLAS. Would you like a drink, Patrick?

PATRICK. I'll get it. (*Goes to the bar and fixes himself a drink*) Doug, you left the office early today.

DOUGLAS. I had some things to do before I came here tonight. Did those perfume shipments go out on time?

PATRICK. Yes, the shipments went out on time.

DOUGLAS. All 175?

PATRICK. All 175.

DOUGLAS. I'd better not find any in the warehouse tomorrow. I don't want those Beverly Hills princesses breathing down my neck again.

PATRICK. They all went out, okay? I told you I could handle it.

DOUGLAS. Don't be so damned cocky. You've only been a

supervisor for two months.

PATRICK. Yeah, and I haven't screwed up anything yet, have I?

DOUGLAS. Let's see how long you can keep it that way.

PATRICK. God, man, I thought Dad made me feel useless. You make him sound like my number one fan.

DOUGLAS. You're not exactly executive material, you know. That's one thing you didn't inherit from your father.

PATRICK. You're complimenting him? I'd like to get this on tape.

DOUGLAS. Don't be such a smart ass. I may disagree with 90 percent of everything he does, but after 50 years the business is still going strong, and he ran it alone for 20 years before he bribed me into joining him.

PATRICK. Why *did* you suddenly join up with him?

DOUGLAS. I had no choice.

PATRICK. How come?

DOUGLAS. Let's just say that your father can be very persuasive. Remember how he suckered you into working for him?

PATRICK. Remember? I'll never forgive him for that.

DOUGLAS. It's not easy to say no to him though, is it?

PATRICK. No kidding! But what could I do? If I didn't change my major from Drama to Business, he would have cut me off. So I learned his stupid business so that when you two kick off I can run it.

DOUGLAS. Into the ground.

PATRICK. Well, neither one of you will be here to stop me.

DOUGLAS. That's your plan, isn't it? Once you get ahold of the business, you're just going to destroy it – or even worse, sell it.

(**PATRICK** *smiles and enters the kitchen.*)

ARLENE. I didn't know we were going to be playing "Truth or Dare" tonight.

DOUGLAS. Arlene, every time this family gets together, it's a game of "Truth or Dare."

ARLENE. True.

COLLEEN. *(Enters from the kitchen)* Dinner is ready.

KATIE. I'll go get Dad.

COLLEEN. I'll help you.

(**COLLEEN** *and* **KATIE** *exit to Shannon's room.*)

KATIE. Grab your tap shoes. It's show time.

SHANNON. You're not going to let me get out of this, are you?

KATIE. Nope. (**KATIE** *and* **COLLEEN** *help* **SHANNON** *out of bed and into a wheelchair.*) Come on. We'll all be together except Sharon, and hopefully she'll get here before dessert.

SHANNON. Colleen, tell her I shouldn't be getting out of bed.

KATIE. Don't expect Colleen to come to your rescue.

COLLEEN. That's right. You need to sit up for a while. You've been in bed all day today.

SHANNON. I'm tired.

COLLEEN. Come on. Let's go.

SHANNON. You're a cruel woman, Colleen McCarthy.

COLLEEN. That's why you love me so much.

SHANNON. Is that why? *(To* **KATIE***)* And you, you're just as bad.

KATIE. *(To* **COLLEEN***)* I sure am glad you're on my side.

COLLEEN. Likewise.

SHANNON. I really do love you two.

KATIE. We love you too, Dad.

COLLEEN. We sure do.

KATIE. Come on. Let's get this show on the road. At this rate, Sharon will get there before we do.

SHANNON. She is coming alone, isn't she? I hope she doesn't bring any of her gypsy friends with her.

KATIE. No. She knows this dinner is for the family only.

SHANNON. Good. *(Laughs)* Maybe she'll call up Leonardo D'Vinci on that psychic hot line of hers and get him to come and do a portrait. He's good at last supper scenes.

KATIE. If anyone could do it, Sharon could.

SHANNON. She's still messing with that blasphemous spook stuff, isn't she?

KATIE. Oh yeah. She has a séance every time there's a full moon and on the night of every Friday the 13th.

COLLEEN. Who does she try to contact?

KATIE. I don't know. I've never been to one of her little parties.

SHANNON. You always were the smart one.

COLLEEN. Sit up nice and tall.

KATIE. And no dribble tricks tonight.

SHANNON. I'll be a perfect gentleman.

(KATIE wheels SHANNON out into the dining room and puts him at the head of the table. DOUGLAS, KATIE, PATRICK, and ARLENE sit at the table. EVERYONE bows their heads and folds their hands.)

SHANNON. Oh Lord, bless us and the food we are about to eat. And let us get through this meal without killing each other.

ARLENE. Touching.

SHANNON. *(Raises his glass.)* May your troubles be few and far between like the space between your grandmother's teeth. *(Looks around at everyone.)* It's been a long time since we've all been together.

ARLENE. Too long.

(Said simultaneously.)

DOUGLAS. Not long enough.

KATIE. Why don't we try to have a nice, pleasant meal. It won't take long, and then you can all go back to being yourselves.

SHANNON. Well said.

> (**COLLEEN** *enters with a tray full of meat and puts it in the middle of the table and Enters the kitchen. Everyone begins serving themselves and eating.*)

ARLENE. I'd like to hear what everybody's been doing lately. Katie?

KATIE. Not much. I pay the bills and read a lot and play chess with Dad. I go to a movie once in a while, when there's one worth seeing.

SHANNON. She baby sits me is what she does. This little lass has given up her job and hardly ever sees her friends just so she can take care of her poor old gray-haired father.

KATIE. It's not as bad as he makes it sound. I go out enough, and *(To* SHANNON:*)* I love taking care of you.

SHANNON. I'd be lost without you, Katie me darlin'.

ARLENE. Douglas?

DOUGLAS. *(Bitterly)* I work.

ARLENE. That's it?

DOUGLAS. That's it.

SHANNON. You're full of malarkey.

DOUGLAS. Why don't you keep your mouth shut!

KATIE. So much for our nice pleasant meal.

DOUGLAS. You think it's easy running that business by myself?

SHANNON. I did it for 20 years.

DOUGLAS. That was 30 years ago, Shannon. In case you haven't notice, things have changed since then. We have 20 times as many customers as we had back then, and *(Pointing to* PATRICK*)* 100 times as many headaches.

PATRICK. Hey, it wasn't my idea to become a prisoner of O'Leary Enterprises.

DOUGLAS. Prisoner? You're lucky to have that job. There are a lot of people out of work today, you know, people who would give anything to have a job like yours.

PATRICK. Hey, they can have it. I never wanted it.

SHANNON. Lad, you're an O'Leary whether you like it or not, and this is the family business, and being a male member of this family, it is your duty to be a part of the business as well.

PATRICK. No choice.

SHANNON. That's right, son. You're either with us or agin' us.

PATRICK. I'll take a Guinness.

DOUGLAS. Don't be such a smart ass. This business has given you a lot of privileges most boys never get.

PATRICK. It's a privilege to have to spend my life doing something I don't want to do?

SHANNON. And what is it that you wanted to do? *(Pause)* Ah yes, that's right. You wanted to become a famous actor, another Lawrence Olivier.

PATRICK. *Sir* Lawrence Olivier.

DOUGLAS. Yes, now you get knighted for playing dress up and pretending to be someone you're not.

PATRICK. Acting is an honorable profession.

SHANNON. Honorable, you say?

PATRICK. Yeah. Lots of actors and actresses are very well respected – Sir Anthony Hopkins, Robert DeNiro, Dame Judith Dench.

SHANNON. Eddie Murphy? America's version of Black Irish.

PATRICK. What about Bill Cosby? You like him. You even read his book.

SHANNON. Surely I did. I read all about the joys of fatherhood, according to Mr. Bill Cosby. Best piece of fiction I've ever read – more like science fiction.

KATIE. Not for most families.

SHANNON. In case you haven't noticed darlin', we're not like most families. *(To **PATRICK**)* Why don't you tell your Mother what else you've been doing.

PATRICK. I've been seeing someone lately.

ARLENE. *(Delighted)* Oh really? What's she like?

SHANNON. *(To Arlene)* You're going to love this.

PATRICK. She's beautiful. She sings. She's divorced and has a little girl, two years old. She's an intern at New York Memorial Hospital, and she's a vegetarian.

ARLENE. Is she Catholic?

PATRICK. *(Pause)* She's Dr. Goldberg's daughter, Sarah.

ARLENE. Holy Mother of God! You're not serious about her, are you?

PATRICK. Very.

ARLENE. This is your fault, Shannon!

SHANNON. Why is this my fault?

ARLENE. You had to have a Jewish doctor.

SHANNON. They're the best.

ARLENE. No, they're the most expensive.

SHANNON. That's because they're the best.

ARLENE. A lot of good he's doing you!

SHANNON. Now don't go blaming my dying on Dr. Goldberg. He's seen our family through three births, two deaths and more colds than you've got gray hairs hiding under that red.

ARLENE. I've never understood why you stay with that quack. He's charging you a fortune, not making you any better, and now this!

PATRICK. Mother, shut up! Dr. Goldberg is a wonderful man, and Sarah is smarter, sweeter, and a far better person than anyone in this family will ever be.

SHANNON. Now I know why God hasn't blessed me with grandchildren. Who can blame him for not wanting to continue this chapter of the O'Learys.

PATRICK. Cheer up, Dad. Sarah and I will give you plenty of grandchildren someday.

ARLENE. That's not funny, Patrick. *(Pause)* Tell me something, son. What are you celebrating this month,

Christmas or Hanukkah?

PATRICK. Both.

ARLENE. And what kind of carols will you be singing? "Deck the Halls with Matzo Balls?"

PATRICK. Very funny, Mother.

KATIE. Why don't we all just shut up and finish our meal in peace.

SHANNON. Good idea.

(*The lights go down to indicate time passing. The door-bell rings.*)

COLLEEN. (*From the hallway where she has obviously been eaves-dropping*) I'll get it. (*Opens the door.* **SHARON** *enters.*) Hi Sharon. Come on in. They're still eating dinner.

SHARON. (*Stops suddenly as she enters the dining room*) Oh my God! I wish I had a camera.

COLLEEN. Why don't you sit down. I'll get you a plate. (*Exits to the kitchen*)

ARLENE. (*Gets up and hugs Sharon*) Sharon, how are you?

SHARON. Apparently much better than you. (*Hugs Arlene again*) You're tense. You're worried about (*Pause*) your cats, but don't be. They're fine. And you're up to something, Mother. What is it?

ARLENE. Sharon, stop that clairvoyant, mind reading crap and sit down. I haven't seen you in over a year, so let's wait for at least a little while before we start getting on each other's nerves. Besides, you'd be tense too if you'd been on the airplane ride from Hell that I was on today.

(**SHARON** *laughs and sits at the empty seat next to* **ARLENE.** **COLLEEN** *enters with a plate and silverware and puts it in front of* **SHARON.**)

SHARON. What happened? (*Begins serving herself and eating*)

ARLENE. I'll tell you all about it later. I want to hear about you now. How's your business doing?

SHARON. Business is good. I have a new supplier for my beads. I brought some samples. I'll show you later.

ARLENE. *(Playing with one of Sharon's earrings)* Do you sell a lot of these?

SHARON. Enough to pay the bills. How are you feeling, Dad?

SHANNON. I'm still here.

SHARON. You sure are. See? I told you God wouldn't strike you down with a bolt of lightning if you got the whole family together in one room.

SHANNON. The day isn't over yet, darlin'.

SHARON. Oh, come on. Everything's gonna be just fine – including you. *(Takes Shannon's hand and closes her eyes)* I can see you being with us for a long, long time.

(EVERYONE except KATIE, SHARON, and SHANNON looks around at each other trying to disguise their horror at the thought.)

PATRICK. And if Sharon can see it, it must be true.

KATIE. *(Smiles at SHARON and raises her glass.)* I'll drink to that.

(EVERYONE raises their glasses. KATIE, SHARON, and SHANNON are smiling genuinely, and ARLENE, DOUGLAS, and PATRICK have worried, forced smiles.)

SHANNON. Might I have a word with all of you while we're here together?

PATRICK. About what?

SHANNON. About my wake, lad.

ARLENE. Shannon, not now. That's not appropriate conversation for the dinner table.

SHANNON. Balderdash! I could go at any time now, and I want to make sure that instructions are given while I'm still among the living to give them.

PATRICK. Why don't you wait till after and let Sharon call you up?

SHARON. Non-believers are such a pain in the butt.

SHANNON. When it's over and I'm gone, I want things to be run as if I was here supervising, and I will be. Arlene, a corpse is woman's work. I want you and the girls to dress me in my blue suit with a light blue shirt and plain white tie.

SHARON. Dad, not now.

ARLENE. You don't want to wear your tux?

SHANNON. I wouldn't be caught dead wearing that thing for all eternity. The blue suit will be fine. Douglas, you're in charge of the bar. You're to bring up ten bottles of my best whiskey from the cellar. That'll get you through the day.

DOUGLAS. Very nicely.

SHANNON. Patrick, you're to give each mourner a pinch of salt to put in their pocket.

PATRICK. No way.

SHANNON. Look, you heathen, I'm still the head of this family, and as long as I am, you'll do what I'm telling you.

PATRICK. You're gonna get a nice, normal wake. It's not going to be a freak show like Grandpa Donnley's.

SHANNON. It will be exactly like Grandpa Donnley's! I came into this world an Irishman, and I'm going out an Irishman, in the true Irish spirit. And you'll give everyone a pinch of salt like I told you to. There'll be no evil spirits at this wake.

PATRICK. Let Sharon do that. That's right up her alley.

SHANNON. I'm telling you to do it, lad.

PATRICK. Man, people are gonna think we're nuts!

SHANNON. To hell with what people think! This is my wake, and it'll be done my way or I won't die.

KATIE. Don't worry, Dad. Everything will be done just the way you want it.

SHANNON. You girls make sure the candles burn brightly and that my new boots are by my feet so I can walk right through Purgatory and straight to the gates of Heaven. And don't forget my rosary.

KATIE. It'll be on your hands as if you're saying it with us.

SHANNON. Colleen! Quit your eavesdropping and get in here.

(**COLLEEN** *enters.*)

SHANNON. You've got your work cut out for you too. You're to make a lamb stew, potato bread and soda bread, with butter, and blood pudding. No, maybe not. Knowing these people, they'd probably use my own blood. Get some Limerick bacon and ham. They're the best. And cheese, blarney cheese, and lots of it.

PATRICK. This is insane!

SHANNON. No, boy, this is Irish. I'm a lace curtain Irishman, and I want everyone to know it. Now, about the Will. Arlene, I've made you my executor.

ARLENE. Executrix.

SHANNON. Whatever.

DOUGLAS. Why Arlene? A man should be in charge of the Will.

SHARON. Uncle Doug, join the 21st century.

DOUGLAS. A man is always in charge of the Will.

ARLENE. That's not true. If it were, they never would have invented the word, "executrix."

DOUGLAS. Executrix. Sounds like a hooker for businessmen. Why are you doing this, Shannon?

SHANNON. When we were first married, Arlene handled all the money and did the bookkeeping for the business. She's a wiz with numbers.

DOUGLAS. But you always complained because she spent too much money.

SHANNON. That was our own money. When it came to the business, she knew just when to spend and when to save. She'll treat the Will as if it was business.

ARLENE. And you all know that I will handle things fairly and carry out the Will just as Shannon has written it.

SHANNON. That's right. And I don't want any disputing of the Will. You'll all take what you get and be happy with it. I want the reading of the Will to be on the first night of the wake when only the family is here.

ARLENE. You mean the family and your attorney.

SHANNON. Of course, but if Sol is out of town or for some reason can't be there, Arlene has permission to read the Will to you. *(Pause)* Katie, darlin', I'm getting sleepy. Could you be a sweetheart and bring me back to my room?

KATIE. Sure.

(**KATIE** *wheels* **SHANNON** *back to his room and helps him into bed.*)

KATIE. I hated listening to you talk about your wake and your Will.

SHANNON. I know, but it has to be done. If I don't tell these knuckleheads how to do all this, they'll make a mess of the whole shebang.

(**COLLEEN** *enters the dining room and begins clearing off the table.* **ARLENE, SHARON, DOUGLAS,** *and* **PATRICK** *exit to the living room.*)

KATIE. Goodnight, Dad. Pleasant dreams. *(Kisses* **SHANNON***)*

SHANNON. Katie, could you call Dr. Goldberg and ask him to come over for a bit?

KATIE. Sure. You rest comfortably till he gets here. *(Enters the hall)*

ARLENE. Well, what shall we do?

PATRICK. We already tried talking.

SHARON. Let's play a game.

DOUGLAS. We've already done that, too.

ARLENE. Look we're a family. Let's try to act like one. I really did come here to make peace with Shannon. Why don't we all try to get along like we used to.

(Nobody responds.)

How long do you think we're all going to be here?

DOUGLAS. Could be a while. Could be a week or two.

PATRICK. Could be longer.

DOUGLAS. Could be shorter. *(Pause)* I mean, anything can happen.

ARLENE. That's right. Life's a funny thing. One minute you're here, and the next minute you're gone.

PATRICK. Then, before you know it, there's nobody alive who even knew you ever existed.

SHARON. That's only temporary. Those who were interrupted by death before their time, return to finish what they were sent here to do. These souls get another chance to live a better life, and to do something worth being remembered for so they are not forgotten.

PATRICK. Yeah, right. *(Pause)* Do you think the old man is suffering much?

DOUGLAS. It's hard to tell with him.

ARLENE. People shouldn't have to suffer needlessly. Too bad that doctor he loves so much can't do anything to *(Pause)* help him. You know, last week on my soap, there was an Angel of Mercy at the hospital. She was helping the terminally ill patients find peace.

DOUGLAS. It takes a special kind of doctor to do that. I don't think Dr. Goldberg is the type.

ARLENE. I wasn't suggesting that he was – or should be.

SHARON. Of course not.

DOUGLAS. Besides, like I said, anything can happen.

PATRICK. That's right. Most accidents do happen in the home.

DOUGLAS. That's what they say. Somebody could fall out of bed and hit his head on a nightstand or something.

PATRICK. People accidentally get the wrong medication, or too much.

ARLENE. Or not enough.

DOUGLAS. Wheelchairs can suddenly go berserk.

ARLENE. Someone could fall out of a chair and roll down the hall, out the front door, down the flight of stairs outside, right into the street and get run over by a car.

(**EVERYBODY** *looks at her.*)

ARLENE. It could happen.

SHARON. Would you listen to yourselves? I don't believe what I'm hearing.

ARLENE. We're just having fun, Sharon.

PATRICK. Yeah, lighten up.

DOUGLAS. Yeah, besides, life is very unpredictable. That's why those of us who still have long lives ahead of us should do anything in our power to make our lives as enjoyable as possible. We owe it to ourselves.

(*They all look at each other in silence thinking about what has just been said.*)

KATIE. *(Enters)* What do we owe to ourselves?

SHARON. To enjoy life.

KATIE. You're right. *(Pause)* I just called Dr. Goldberg. He's on his way over.

DOUGLAS. *(Hopefully)* Should we call Father Hammond?

KATIE. No. You're going to have to wait for that.

(**DOUGLAS** *looks disappointed. He goes over to the bar and fixes himself a drink.*)

ARLENE. You know, as long as we're all together, maybe this would be a good time to start planning (*Pause as two chords are heard played from an organ, soap opera style*) the arrangements.

KATIE. You mean?

ARLENE. Yes. That way, when the time comes, we won't be rushed and forget something and we can do everything just right. (*Goes to a desk and takes out some paper and a pen and begins writing what is being said*)

DOUGLAS. Makes sense to me.

ARLENE. Okay, who wants to order the flowers for the house?

SHARON. I'll do that. I know a great florist on Mulberry Street. (*Takes a card out of her purse and reads:*) ''Flowers for all occasions from cradle to grave.''

ARLENE. *(Yells to kitchen)* Colleen, come in here.

COLLEEN. *(Enters)* Yes, Mrs. O'Leary?

ARLENE. You should be in here too. We're discussing *(Pause as the chords are heard again)* the arrangements.

COLLEEN. I've got the menu Mr. O'Leary asked me to prepare.

ARLENE. Do you understand everything he wants?

COLLEEN. Yes, Mrs. O'Leary.

PATRICK. Make sure you get some Corn Critters too, okay?

SHARON. Yeah, and some Potato Poopies.

COLLEEN. Okay.

KATIE. This isn't a party!

DOUGLAS. You obviously don't remember Grandpa Donn-ley's wake.

ARLENE. What about drinks?

DOUGLAS. I'm in charge of drinks, remember?

ARLENE. That's right. Who wants to pick out the casket?

PATRICK. I'll do that.

(**COLLEEN** *goes to the kitchen.*)

ARLENE. Get the best one they have. Make sure it's airtight and waterproof.

PATRICK. Should it be soundproof too?

ARLENE. Just get the best. I'll pick out the headstone.

KATIE. What are you going to have them put on it?

(**ARLENE, PATRICK, DOUGLAS** *and* **SHARON** *look at each other like they're trying to think of something clever.*)

PATRICK. How about: My time's run out,

But there's no doubt.

I can still rant and rave

Though I'm down in this grave.

DOUGLAS. I've got one: From Cork to New York

Came an Irish dork.

I was once a six foot wonder.

Now I'm six feet under.

ARLENE. Wait a minute. How's this:

> Beloved husband – that's a laugh.
> I made my lovely wife go daft.
> My work came first, and to her that sucked,
> But I didn't care, cause she was …

KATIE. Mother! I think you've had enough to drink. *(Takes Arlene's drink out of her hand)* Stop it! All of you! Can't any of you find it in your heart to make peace with a dying old man?

DOUGLAS. Any other dying old man, sure.

KATIE. You know, if it wasn't for the fact that he started O'Leary Enterprises, the company that you all hate so much, you wouldn't be on the verge of inheriting over $1,000,000 each. Can't you at least think of it that way and be a little grateful?

PATRICK. I'll be grateful when I get the money.

DOUGLAS. That's right. Until I have that money in my hand, I don't trust him, and I'm not grateful to him.

ARLENE. You've got a point. None of us even knows for sure that we're in his Will.

SHARON. That's why you came here today, Mother, isn't it – to make sure you're in his Will?

ARLENE. Of course not, Sharon. I wanted to make peace with him. I couldn't live with myself if he died and we were still on bad terms.

KATIE. So this is all for your peace of mind.

ARLENE. Sure. After he's dead, he won't care.

(The doorbell rings.)

KATIE. But you'll still be alive to feel guilty.

ARLENE. And you know I would. *(Softly)* I'm very sensitive.

(The doorbell rings again.)

ARLENE. *(Yells to the kitchen)* Colleen, answer the damned door!

KATIE. *(Calls to the kitchen)* I'll get it, Colleen. *(Opens the door)* Come in, Dr. Goldberg.

DR. GOLDBERG. *(Enters)* Hello, Katie.

ARLENE. Dr. Goldberg.

DR. GOLDBERG. Arlene, it's been a long time.

ARLENE. At least ten years.

DR. GOLDBERG. How have you been?

ARLENE. Wonderful. California's been very good to me.

DR. GOLDBERG. I can see that.

ARLENE. *(Upset)* How's your daughter, Sarah?

DR. GOLDBERG. I'd better go see what Shannon wants.

KATIE. *(Follows* **DR. GOLDBERG** *into Shannon's room)* It's getting harder for him to breathe.

*(***KATIE*** and* **DR. GOLDBERG** *enter Shannon's room and close the door.)*

SHARON. Now, where were we? Oh yes, the tombstone. If we're going to have it blessed by Father Hammond, we'd better be serious. Let's just go with beloved ex-husband, father, and brother.

*(***SHARON*** takes Arlene's paper from her and writes on it.)*

ARLENE. Beloved ex-husband? I don't think so.

*(***ARLENE*** takes the paper back from* **SHARON** *and scratches it out.)*

DOUGLAS. Don't worry about "brother." You can leave that off too.

*(***KATIE*** enters.)*

ARLENE. Are you sure?

DOUGLAS. Beloved brother?

ARLENE. *(Scratches out "brother")* Well, I want to be represented on there somehow.

SHARON. Then how about, "Beloved Father and Friend"?

ARLENE. Perfect.

DR. GOLDBERG. *(Enters the living room)* It's over.

End of Act One

ACT TWO

*(The living room is overdone with flowers and candles. There is a long table in the middle of the room covered with food and the bar has ten bottles of Irish whiskey on it. **COLLEEN** is finishing rearranging the furniture. There is a little table in front of the Christmas tree with a black tablecloth and two white candles. The couch is facing away from this table. There are two chairs in front of the couch, one that is facing the small table in the back and one facing away from the table. **COLLEEN** exits and returns with **SHANNON** dressed in a blue suit in his wheelchair.)*

COLLEEN. I don't know how you expect to pull this off. You've done some crazy things in your days, but this.

SHANNON. Hey, it's worked so far. Nobody even questioned you when you offered to take care of the body and get me all gussied up for this farewell party. Besides, they never paid any attention to me before. Why should they start now?

COLLEEN. What about Katie?

SHANNON. She's the only one I feel bad about doing this to.

COLLEEN. She's never going to forgive you for not letting her in on this.

SHANNON. I couldn't take that chance. Not that I don't trust her, but I knew she would have been against the idea of me faking my death.

COLLEEN. And she would have been right. I ought to have my head examined for going along with this.

SHANNON. I knew you would though. You've got a spark of the devil in you that wouldn't be able to resist these kinds of shenanigans. *(Takes Colleen's hand)* You're my special lady. You're always there for me.

COLLEEN. I never could say no to you. But Doc Goldberg? I'm really surprised he went along with this, although the two of you together always have been like the Odd Couple. How is he getting away with it though? This is highly unethical.

SHANNON. Unethical? He's the best damned doctor in the country. Don't you be calling him unethical!

COLLEEN. Now don't get your spizerinctom in an uproar. I just don't want anyone to get in trouble over this.

SHANNON. You leave my spizerinctom out of this. And quit worrying so much. Nobody's going to be getting into any trouble.

COLLEEN. Not until Katie finds out what you've done. She'll be fit to be tied when she finds out you let her think you were dead. I just hope she doesn't hate me for lying to her.

SHANNON. Don't you worry about Katie. She'll be just fine, especially when she finds out why I did it.

COLLEEN. What are you going to tell her? How are you going to explain this to everyone?

SHANNON. You always hear about how relatives go off half cocked when the head of the family dies and leaves them a lot of money. Nobody is ever satisfied. Everybody wants more. This is my chance to find out who deserves what, so that when the time really does come, things will be done right.

COLLEEN. Well, I'd better get you situated here. They'll be back any minute.

(**COLLEEN** *helps* **SHANNON** *into the chair at the little table.*)

SHANNON. Don't forget my rosary.

COLLEEN. I've got your rosary. (*Takes a rosary out of her pocket and gives it to* **SHANNON.**)

SHANNON. You got my boots?

COLLEEN. I've got your boots. (*Takes a pair of boots from under the little table and puts them next to Shannon's feet* *on the outside of the table)* All the food's out and there's plenty of whiskey.

SHANNON. Good. They'll need it. And so will I.

COLLEEN. You? You're not going to sit back here and drink.

SHANNON. And why not?

COLLEEN. You'll get caught for sure.

SHANNON. Don't worry. They won't see me. They'll have their backs to me anyway. You make sure they all sit on the couch. You sit in the chair where I can see you in case anything goes wrong.

COLLEEN. What do you mean in case anything goes wrong?

SHANNON. Don't worry. Nothing's going to go wrong. I just want to make sure, that's all.

COLLEEN. Don't worry. Don't worry. How can you say, "Don't worry?"

SHANNON. Because there's nothing to worry about. Just relax and enjoy it. This is going to be the most fun I've had with these people in years.

COLLEEN. I just wish you would have agreed to lie in a coffin instead of sitting up at a table. They wouldn't go near a coffin, so they wouldn't get a good look at you.

SHANNON. No. This is the way it was done at Grampa Donnley's wake, so this is the way it has to be. Besides, I want to see what's going on and I can't do that lying down.

(Voices are heard off stage at the front door)

COLLEEN. Oh God, they're here.

SHANNON. As Katie would say, it's show time!

COLLEEN. Good luck. *(Kisses SHANNON on the forehead and starts to walk away, taking the wheelchair with her. She stops, turns and points to SHANNON)* Play dead.

(SHANNON and COLLEEN laugh. COLLEEN goes to the kitchen. The front door opens and KATIE, ARLENE, DOUGLAS, SHARON, and PATRICK enter.)

KATIE. Colleen?

COLLEEN. (*Enters from the kitchen*) Hi. How was the rosary?

KATIE. It went well. I'm glad you suggested having only the family here on the first night of the wake. I don't feel like dealing with a lot of people tonight.

COLLEEN. What we all need is a quiet evening at home to emotionally prepare for all the visitors coming tomorrow.

PATRICK. Colleen, this family has never had a quiet evening at home.

DOUGLAS. (*Looking at* SHANNON.) Maybe now we can.

KATIE. Anyway, it'll be nice to have some time alone with Father. (*Looks around the living room*) You did a beautiful job setting things up.

COLLEEN. Thanks.

PATRICK. Yeah, it looks great. (*Starts picking at the food.*)

DOUGLAS. So, where's the Will?

ARLENE. I'll go get it.

(DOUGLAS, PATRICK, *and* SHARON *sit on the couch.*)

COLLEEN. (*To* KATIE) Why don't you sit here with your brother and sister? I'll sit over here. (KATIE *sits on the couch and* COLLEEN *sits in the chair facing* SHANNON.)

ARLENE. (*Enters and sits in the other chair*) Colleen, I see no reason for you to be here. This is a family matter.

(COLLEEN *starts to get up.* SHANNON *raises his hand as if to tell* COLLEEN *to stop.* COLLEEN *sits down.*)

COLLEEN. Maybe I should stay.

KATIE. Good. I want you to stay.

ARLENE. Colleen.

(COLLEEN, *looking very nervous, starts to get up. Shannon's hand goes up again.* COLLEEN *sits.*)

KATIE. Mother, she's staying.

ARLENE. All right, all right.

PATRICK. Let's just get on with it.

ARLENE. Since your father's lawyer is away on business, I, *(looking at* DOUGLAS *as if to rub it in)* as executrix, will read the Will. *(Pause – Begins reading.)* I, Shannon Joseph O'Leary, being of sound mind and body, blah, blah, blah.

KATIE. Mother, read it right.

ARLENE. Well, the damned thing goes on forever.

DOUGLAS. Kind of like the person who wrote it.

(SHANNON *flips* DOUGLAS *off.* COLLEEN *covers her mouth to hide her laughing.)*

KATIE. Uncle Doug!

DOUGLAS. Sorry.

ARLENE. Anyway, you don't really want to hear all this legal mumbo-jumbo.

PATRICK. Yeah, skip to the good stuff.

ARLENE. *(Scanning the Will)* Okay, here we go. I'd like the stocks of O'Leary Enterprises that are not owned by the Corporation to be put into a trust divided equally among my children, Katheryn Margaret, Sharon Margaret, and Patrick Joseph and my ex-wife, Arlene Margaret, and my brother, Douglas Joseph.

PATRICK. A trust? Does that mean that we're not going to get any money from his stupid business until we're old and decrepit like him?

ARLENE. That's what it means. And I'll be damned if I'm going to come all the way out here from California just to be put in a trust!

DOUGLAS. You? I've worked my butt off for that damned company for the last 20 years. I'll fight this if I have to take it all the way the goddamned Supreme Court!

PATRICK. What about me? I gave up a chance at an acting career to count nuts and bolts in a hell hole of a stock-room for him.

KATIE. Relax, Patrick. You make a good salary. You have plenty to live on.

PATRICK. Don't you talk to me about work. You haven't had

a job in two years.

COLLEEN. She's worked damned hard taking care of your father and this house!

*(**SHANNON** gestures as if cheering.)*

ARLENE. Colleen!

KATIE. Colleen, don't worry about it.

DOUGLAS. Screw this part of the Will. We'll deal with this once Sol gets back in town. What else does the jerk have to say?

ARLENE. *(Continues reading)* Douglas, you will continue running the business until you retire or go nuts, which ever comes first. At that time, God help me, the company will be turned over to my son, Patrick, who I hope by then has learned the value of a dollar and the importance of being a respectable Irishman who proudly carries on the family business.

*(**PATRICK** snickers.)*

ARLENE. *(Reading)* The dividends from your shares of the stock will not make you rich, but they will help you live comfortably. Of course, if you're smart, you'll let them roll over to buy more shares, so that when you retire, you'll be set for life.

PATRICK. If we're smart! Oh, please! Where is Sol?

COLLEEN. He's on vacation. He'll be back next week.

ARLENE. At this rate, I'm not going to get home for at least another two weeks! This is outrageous!

KATIE. It's nice to see you too, Mother.

ARLENE. Don't get smart with me, little girl!

KATIE. I'm not your little girl!

ARLENE. You never were, were you? You were always Daddy's precious little twit.

KATIE. Why don't you shut up, Mother!

ARLENE. Why don't you shut up!

SHARON. Why don't both of you shut up!

ARLENE. Sharon!

SHARON. I'm sorry, Mother, but I can't stand all this yelling.

KATIE. You know she has that effect on me.

ARLENE. That's a lovely way to talk about your mother.

KATIE. What do you expect? You come out here just to suck up to Dad so you can make sure you're in his Will and then you cause nothing but trouble.

ARLENE. Look, let's just get this over with, okay?

KATIE. I'm sorry. Go on.

ARLENE. *(Reading)* Now, I have a puzzle for you all to solve.

PATRICK. What?

ARLENE. *(Reading)* The clues are in the presents I leave to each of you.

DOUGLAS. Oh, this is asinine!

KATIE. I love it! He's still playing games.

COLLEEN. Right to the end.

SHARON. And beyond.

ARLENE. *(Reading)* To Sharon, my little gypsy girl. You probably won't admit it, but I bet you're going to miss having me make fun of your little spook sessions. Just do me one favor. If you try looking for me in that crystal ball of yours, don't expect me to come entertain you and your friends. Let's really put those so-called powers to a test. My gift to you is a chance to prove once and for all whether these powers are for real or if you're just full of blarney. Tune into your little psychic channel and see what you find, and what you don't find. And when you figure it out, remember to consider the probability and the outcome.

SHARON. What?

ARLENE. That's it.

SHARON. I don't get it. *(Pause)* Wait a minute – the probability and the outcome. Where have I heard that before? *(Pause)* The probability and the outcome. I know where I've heard that. That's from the movie, *Heaven Can Wait*. Warren Beatty talks about the probability and the outcome of what happens after you die.

KATIE. What's that got to do with you?

SHARON. I don't know. Dad and I watched *Heaven Can Wait* a few times in the last couple of years because we both like it so much, but I'm not sure what it means here.

PATRICK. Well, plug yourself in and see what your ghost friends tell you.

SHARON. Don't worry. I'll figure it out.

ARLENE. Let's go on. *(Reading)* To Patrick, my only son. It was harder to think of a present for you than anyone else. You and I are so very different. We may be flesh and blood, but we've always been more like vinegar and water. That's why I wanted your gift to be extra special.

PATRICK. Vinegar and water? We've always been like a douche?

ARLENE. I think he means oil and water.

PATRICK. Maybe – maybe not.

ARLENE. Anyway – *(Reading)* You know that red custom-made Ferrari you keep going down to the garage to drool over? Well, you can't have it. With that lead foot of yours, you'd be dead in a week, and they're not ready for you down there.

PATRICK. Jerk.

ARLENE. *(Reading)* I can hear you calling me all kinds of names right now, boy, but that's okay. There's something else that has to do with drive that I'm leaving you. My gift to you is my ambition. Try speeding on that kind of drive for a change. You have the potential to amount to something, boy, and I'll be damned if I'm going to give up on you now. You and I aren't through yet, son.

PATRICK. Screw you, old man. I don't want any part of your damn business.

ARLENE. Patrick, please. *(Reading)* Douglas, even though I left you in charge of the business, don't think that means that you can run things your own way. I have left strict instructions with the members of the Board to make sure that you continue to take care of the employees in the manner that they are accustomed to. You know how important my loyal employees are to me. I know you've been talking about cutting benefits and salaries lately. If you try this, you will be voted down by the entire Board.

DOUGLAS. He can't do this!

ARLENE. I'm afraid he can. Even the President of the company can't overthrow the Board of Directors. *(Reading)* I leave you this list of promotions and increases in salaries, effective immediately upon my death. My gift to you is the opportunity to be the good guy for a change.

*(**ARLENE** hands **DOUGLAS** a piece of paper. He looks at it and rips it up.)*

DOUGLAS. This is absurd!

ARLENE. *(Reading)* Don't worry. If this copy accidentally gets ripped up or destroyed somehow, I have mailed a copy to each member of the Board with my specific instructions to each one of them and a healthy bonus for carrying out my wishes.

DOUGLAS. *(Turns around and looks at **SHANNON**)* If you weren't already dead.

*(When **DOUGLAS** turns back around facing away from **SHANNON**, **SHANNON** lifts up his glass as if toasting and takes a drink.)*

ARLENE. *(Reading)* Arlene, my wife, my ex-wife, and the mother of my children. Which one of those roles was your favorite? All in all you were a damn good wife. You were even a better ex-wife. And the children all love you, so I guess you did a pretty good job there, too. When you divorced me, you said that along with working too hard, I'd lost my sense of humor. I didn't make you laugh any more. You missed the little practical jokes I used to play on you. You said that when I lost my sense of humor, you lost yours too. Well, I found mine again, and that's my gift to you. Laugh it up, Sweet Cheeks. Life is a joke. For that matter, so is death. So do me a favor. Let out a hardy laugh right now. (**ARLENE** *snickers sarcastically and continues reading.*) And Katie, me darlin'. My dear, sweet Katie.

PATRICK. Here we go. I bet Little Miss Suck-Up gets everything.

KATIE. Patrick!

PATRICK. I'm sorry, Katie.

ARLENE. Can we go on?

PATRICK. Go on.

ARLENE. *(Reading)* You devoted a lot of time to your dear old Dad. I hope you know how much I really appreciate it. I think my favorite part was our daily chess games. My gift to you is something I hope you learned from those games – the ability to not only look out for yourself, but to be able to keep one step ahead of the game at all times, and the insight to read into a rook's plot and to realize the importance of all the players, especially the often forgotten pawn.

PATRICK. What kind of a Will is this? This is so stupid. Why didn't he just give us the money and let us get the hell out of here?

DOUGLAS. He thrives on torturing people. Even from the goddamned grave!

COLLEEN. He's not buried yet.

DOUGLAS. No, but he will be soon.

PATRICK. Not soon enough.

ARLENE. *(Reading)* So, there you have it. I hope you all enjoy your gifts. Don't worry about the rest of my estate. I know none of you are interested in my material possessions, so I'm leaving them all to Colleen McCarthy, my faithful housekeeper.

DOUGLAS, SHARON, ARLENE, & PATRICK. What?

DOUGLAS. This Will is ridiculous! I can't believe Sol even wasted his time drawing it up.

KATIE. *(Laughing)* Dad, only you could do this.

ARLENE. *(Reading)* Colleen, I hope they had the good sense to include you in on the reading of the Will so you're hearing this first hand and getting the pleasure of watching their reactions. And don't let that pack of thieves rob you blind before they leave. They'll steal the gold in your teeth if you don't watch out. But if there is anything here you don't need or don't want to keep, you can give it away as you see fit. In closing, I just want to say, it's been a hell of a life, and at the very least, you all made it quite interesting. Goodbye for now. *(Looks at everyone)* That's it.

DOUGLAS. This is the most outrageous thing I've ever heard!

ARLENE. I promise you, the minute Sol gets back into town, I will make sure that this so-called Will is null and void!

PATRICK. I want my money!

SHARON. Wait a minute. Remember how Dad used to joke about a hidden treasure in the house?

KATIE. He was just kidding.

PATRICK. Are you sure?

KATIE. Of course. He would never hide anything of value.

DOUGLAS. I don't know. The old miser just might have planted something so no one would ever find it.

COLLEEN. Look, I've been cleaning this house from top to bottom for over 15 years. I would know if there was any hidden treasure.

ARLENE. Don't worry. We'll all get our money as soon as Sol gets back into town.

KATIE. You've waited this long. You can wait one more week.

ARLENE. All right. In the meantime, what's this puzzle we're supposed to figure out?

KATIE. Who knows?

PATRICK. Who cares?

DOUGLAS. Yeah, who cares about the damned puzzle? All I

can figure out is that the stiff stiffed us.

SHARON. Look, I know you all think I'm crazy and you don't believe in my powers, but just for the hell of it, why don't we have a séance. If I can contact Dad, we can ask him about the puzzle clues.

DOUGLAS. Screw the puzzle clues! I want to talk to that son-of-a-bitch about the whole damned Will!

PATRICK. Yeah, me too!

SHARON. Then you'll do this with me?

(**EVERYBODY** *looks at each other inquisitively.*)

PATRICK. Oh hell, why not? Nothing else to do tonight. Besides, we need a good laugh.

SHARON. Great! Colleen, will you help me get the room ready?

COLLEEN. You bet. I wouldn't miss this for the world! Why don't you all go into the kitchen and let me and Sharon set everything up.

(**KATIE, PATRICK, DOUGLAS, & ARLENE** *go to the kitchen.* **COLLEEN** *and* **SHARON** *move the food off one of the card tables and move the card table into the middle of the room.* **SHARON** *takes a spray bottle from her purse and sprays the room with it.*)

COLLEEN. What else do we need?

SHARON. Could you bring me one of those candles from Dad's table?

COLLEEN. Sure.

(**COLLEEN** *goes to the table in front of* **SHANNON**. *As she picks up one of the candles,* **SHANNON** *blows out the candle and laughs silently.*)

COLLEEN. So, you really think you'll be able to contact Shannon?

SHARON. I hope so. To tell you the truth, I haven't had very much luck with my séances in the past. But maybe it'll be easier trying to contact someone I know. He might be more responsive than a stranger.

COLLEEN. I think he'll be very responsive.

SHARON. There, we're ready.

COLLEEN. I'll go get the others. *(Goes to the kitchen. Comes out with everyone else.)*

SHARON. Okay, everyone sit down. I'll get the lights. *(Gets a book of matches from a table and hands them to* **KATIE***)* Katie, would you light the candle?

KATIE. Sure.

*(***KATIE*** lights the candle as* **SHARON** *turns off the lights and sits at the table.)*

KATIE. Shouldn't Dad be sitting here with us?

ARLENE. Oh, that's disgusting!

SHARON. No, it's not. That's a good question. But we shouldn't disturb him at this point. He's better off staying just where he is. *(Pause)* Everybody join hands and close your eyes. And please, no jokes or laughing. I know some of you think it's funny, but this is very real, so let's try to get through it without having to start over and over.

DOUGLAS. I don't believe I'm doing this. This is so stupid.

PATRICK. I feel like I'm in a play.

SHARON. Come on. Everybody shut your eyes. I'll tell you when to open them.

(Pause. **SHARON** *recites slowly:)*

Soul of wonder from beyond
Spirits ponder. Called upon
To join the living in our strife
For insight into death's new life.

Rising moon in dark of night,
Answer soon our quest for sight
Into the world we cannot see,
The far side of eternity.

We beckon now to hear our call,
The Specter who will answer all
The mysteries of which we query.

Return to us Shannon O'Leary.

(They sit in silence for a few seconds. A dim light flickers in the back of the room and then goes out. Everyone's eyes are still closed, so no one saw this.)

SHARON. Everybody open your eyes. *(Pause – silence for about five seconds)* Close your eyes again.

(They close their eyes. The light flickers again as they sit in silence.)

SHARON *(Continued)* Father? Are you here? *(Pause)* I know you asked not to be disturbed, so forgive us for not abiding by your wishes. We need to speak to you. *(Pause)* Open your eyes again.

*(There is silence for about five seconds. Then three knocks are heard. **EVERYONE** looks around nervously.)*

SHARON. Oh, my God!

PATRICK. What's wrong?

SHARON. Did you hear that?

KATIE. We all heard that.

ARLENE. What are you so nervous about, Sharon? You do this all the time.

SHARON. Yeah, but this is the first time it's ever worked.

PATRICK. Now she tells us.

DOUGLAS. I'm getting out of here. *(Starts to get up)*

SHARON. No! Nobody move. You'll scare him away.

ARLENE. *We'll* scare *him?*

SHARON. Shh! *(Pause)* Is that you, Dad? *(Pause)* Dad?

*(**KATIE** stands up and sings in Marilyn Monroe's voice.)*

KATIE AS MARILYN. My heart belongs to daddy.

SHARON. Who are you?

KATIE AS MARILYN.. Nobody's daddy, that's for sure.

PATRICK. Marilyn? Marilyn Monroe?

KATIE AS MARILYN. That's right, sugar.

DOUGLAS. Well, I'll be damned.

KATIE AS MARILYN. Oh, honey, be careful what you wish for. You let that happen, and you're gonna miss out on an awful lot of fun. Besides, you'd hate it. It's too hot down there.

PATRICK. Hey, don't forget, Marilyn. Some like it hot.

KATIE AS MARILYN. *(Laughs)* You're cute. What's your name?

PATRICK. Patrick O'Leary.

KATIE AS MARILYN. Well, Patrick O'Leary, how about you and me getting together later? Maybe you can be *my* daddy.

PATRICK. I'd say, "I'm dying to meet you," but you might take me literally.

KATIE AS MARILYN. I'll take you anyway I can get you.

SHARON. Right now, Marilyn, we're looking for *my* daddy.

KATIE AS MARILYN. What's your daddy's name?

SHARON. Shannon O'Leary.

KATIE AS MARILYN. Humm. That's one I haven't met yet.

SHARON. Are you sure?

KATIE AS MARILYN. Sure I'm sure. I wouldn't forget a nice Irish name like that. I'll ask some of my other Irish friends and see if they know him. We'll find him for you.

ARLENE. If you find him, could you tell him we're looking for him?

KATIE AS MARILYN. As long as I don't have to give him back once I find him.

ARLENE. Believe me, you can keep him.

KATIE AS MARILYN. You got a deal.

KATIE sits back down and puts her head on the table for a few seconds as if she's passed out. Then she sits up and looks around at everyone.

ARLENE. *(To PATRICK)* Do you realize you were flirting with a dead woman?

PATRICK. Hey, Marilyn's Marilyn, dead or alive.

> (**SHANNON** *knocks over his drink, breaking the glass.*
> **EVERYONE** *jumps nervously.*)

SHARON. All right, let's try this again. Everyone shut their eyes. *(Pause)* Shannon O'Leary. Please come to us, Shannon O'Leary.

> (**DOUGLAS** *stands and speaks in John Wayne's voice.*)

DOUGLAS AS JOHN. Well, what have we got here?

PATRICK. What the hell? Duke? Is that you?

DOUGLAS AS JOHN. I didn't mean to crash your party, boy.

PATRICK. John Wayne?

DOUGLAS AS JOHN. In the flesh.

PATRICK. Not exactly.

DOUGLAS AS JOHN. You got me there, pilgrim.

PATRICK. How *did* we get you here?

DOUGLAS AS JOHN. I'm a family man from way back. Just can't avoid a family gathering, even if it's not my family.

KATIE. We were looking for our Dad.

DOUGLAS AS JOHN. You look like a real nice bunch. I wish I could say I was him. What are you celebrating down there?

KATIE. Actually, this is his wake.

DOUGLAS AS JOHN. Oh, that's tough, kid. Well, have a couple of swigs and everything'll go down easier.

PATRICK. We've got a head start on that.

DOUGLAS AS JOHN. Good for you, boy.

PATRICK. Too bad you can't join us. We've got plenty of whiskey, rum, scotch.

DOUGLAS AS JOHN. Woah, where is this saloon I've stumbled into?

ARLENE. This is Diamond Rose, New York.

DOUGLAS AS JOHN. And who is this pretty lady?

ARLENE. I'm Mrs. Arlene O'Leary, the widow.

DOUGLAS AS JOHN. Here's to Mrs. O'Leary. What town did

you say this was?

ARLENE. Diamond Rose.

DOUGLAS AS JOHN. Where is that?

ARLENE. Not too far from Manhattan.

DOUGLAS AS JOHN. Never heard of it, ma'am.

ARLENE. It's a relatively new community, very wealthy.

DOUGLAS AS JOHN. Sounds like a nice little town. Hey kids, I'd love to stick around and chat, but I gotta meander.

ARLENE. It was lovely talking to you.

DOUGLAS AS JOHN. Likewise, I'm sure.

ARLENE. Good night, John.

DOUGLAS AS JOHN. Good night to all the lovely O'Learys, and you too, boy.

(*DOUGLAS sits back down and puts his head on the table for a few seconds as if he's passed out. Then he sits up and looks around at everyone.*)

ARLENE. Look, Sharon, this has been very interesting, and actually kind of fun, but let's get down to business here. Can you find Shannon or not?

SHARON. I'm not doing this on purpose. I'm trying to find Dad. I don't know why these people are showing up.

PATRICK. I love it.

DOUGLAS. You would. I wouldn't be surprised if you staged all this.

KATIE. Come on, you two. Let's not get into any of that right now.

SHARON. Yeah, come on. Let's close our eyes again, and this time, concentrate on Dad.

(*A drum is heard, burlesque style.*)

DOUGLAS. What was that?

(*COLLEEN stands and speaks in Mae West's voice.*)

COLLEEN AS MAE. Hi ya, big boy.

EVERYONE. Oh, my God!

KATIE. I can't believe this. Sharon, this is great!

COLLEEN AS MAE. How's everybody doing here tonight?

PATRICK. We're doing great. How are you, Mae?

COLLEEN AS MAE. If it's all the same to you, I prefer Miss West.

PATRICK. Sorry, Miss West.

DOUGLAS. Look, we don't want to talk to you.

ARLENE. Doug, how can you say that to her? This is Mae West you're insulting.

DOUGLAS. Big deal! I never liked her. She was nothing but trash!

COLLEEN AS MAE. I beg your pardon.

PATRICK. Mae West was a lady! A multi-talented lady.

COLLEEN AS MAE. Thank you, dearie.

DOUGLAS. Lady? You just got by on your looks and your wiggle. Those were the only talents you had. I never thought you were any good.

COLLEEN AS MAE. When I'm good, I'm very good. And when I'm bad, I'm better.

DOUGLAS. Look, don't get cute with me. With that mouth of yours, I never understood why you were so successful.

COLLEEN AS MAE. You wouldn't believe what this mouth can do.

DOUGLAS. What's that supposed to mean if you're such a lady?

COLLEEN AS MAE. Why don't you come up and see me sometime, and I'll show you what it means.

DOUGLAS. Get out of here. You go back to the fires of Hell where I'm sure you came from.

COLLEEN AS MAE. Nobody tells me where to go.

DOUGLAS. I'm sure lots of people have told you where to go. And now I'm telling you. No, I'm ordering you. Get out of here!

ARLENE. Douglas, don't talk to her like that!

COLLEEN AS MAE. Yeah, Douglas. Who do you think you are, the master of the house?

DOUGLAS. That's right, Miss West. That's exactly who I am. And it's about time someone ended this so called power you've had over men all these years. Get out of here!

SHARON. Wait a minute, Miss West. Please don't go.

COLLEEN AS MAE. I'm right here, dearie.

SHARON. We really do appreciate you taking the time to come and talk to us, but actually, we're looking for my father. Do you know Shannon O'Leary?

COLLEEN AS MAE. Honey, I know every man up here, but to tell you the truth, that's one I haven't met yet.

ARLENE. Knowing Shannon, he went to find Danny Kaye. He was always his favorite.

KATIE. That's right. Do you know Danny Kaye?

COLLEEN AS MAE. Intimately.

KATIE. Maybe he's seen Dad. Could you ask him for us please?

COLLEEN AS MAE. With pleasure. But I'll warn you. Once I get with Danny, I may not be back.

KATIE. We'll understand.

SHARON. Wait! Before you go, could you send Elvis in?

COLLEEN AS MAE. Elvis?

PATRICK, KATIE, SHARON. Yeah, Elvis Presley.

COLLEEN AS MAE. Honey, Elvis ain't here. We don't expect him for another 5 years.

PATRICK. But Elvis is dead.

COLLEEN AS MAE. Like I said, I know every man up here, and I haven't seen Elvis since Vegas, 1972.

SHARON. Are you sure?

COLLEEN AS MAE. Honey, if there's one thing I'm sure of, it's Vegas, 1972.

KATIE. But Elvis can't be alive.

PATRICK. Yeah. If he's alive, where's he been all these years?

COLLEEN AS MAE. Try 7-11. I've got to run now. The

newcomers just arrived and I'm on the welcoming committee.

DOUGLAS. Go figure.

COLLEEN AS MAE. Good-bye, sweetheart. It's been a real pleasure.

DOUGLAS. Yeah, right.

(**COLLEEN** *sits back down and puts her head on the table for a few seconds as if she's passed out. Then she sits up and looks around at everyone.*)

PATRICK. (*Stands up and sings.*) You ain't nothin' but a hound dog.

PATRICK. (*He stops and looks at everyone.*) Just kidding. (*Sits back down.*)

ARLENE. Very funny, Patrick. Look, Sharon, this could go on all night. We've got some serious business to attend to.

SHARON. I know. Maybe Dad's too new to be able to respond to our calling. You know, he may not be at his final destination yet. If that's the case, we wouldn't be able to contact him until then.

ARLENE. Oh my God! He's in Purgatory!

PATRICK. I'm not saying any Plenary Indulgences to get him out. Let him sit there for a couple millenniums.

ARLENE. Purgatory, mind you. And him with a sure ticket to Hell.

SHARON. We don't know where he is, Mother. Let's just pray for his spirit to guide us in solving the puzzle. We can work out all our other problems with the Will later.

DOUGLAS. I'm getting tired of this nonsense.

SHARON. Okay. Let's just try this one last thing. Everybody say a silent prayer.

PATRICK. Come on, Sharon. Give it up.

SHARON. Now wait a minute everybody. Let's try to solve this thing.

PATRICK. All right, all right. But you go first. Your part of the stupid puzzle is the weirdest.

SHARON. Okay. *(Pause)* Dad, if you can hear me, please help us figure out what you were trying to say.

KATIE. What was that he said, "The probability and the outcome?"

SHARON. Yeah.

KATIE. What's the probability?

SHARON. According to the movie, there were two probabilities. Either he died or he didn't. Those were Warren Beatty's probabilities anyway.

PATRICK. Well, we all know the outcome.

(COLLEEN starts to laugh.)

ARLENE. Colleen, what on earth is so funny?

COLLEEN. I'm sorry. I was just imagining Mr. O'Leary thinking up this puzzle. He must have put a lot of thought into it and had a blast doing it.

PATRICK. I'm glad someone can laugh at this. I think it's a pain in the ass.

DOUGLAS. Do we have to keep holding hands?

SHARON. I guess not. But let's stay here just in case.

ARLENE. In case your father shows up?

SHARON. Yeah.

COLLEEN. I'll be right back. I'm going to clean up that broken glass. *(Exits. Enters with a broom and rag. Sweeps and wipes up the floor by Shannon's table. Fixes him another drink at the bar and puts it in front of him)*

PATRICK. Come on, Katie. You knew him better than anyone. You should be able to figure this out.

KATIE. Hey, I'm just as stumped as the rest of you. What does he mean by, "the often forgotten pawn?" Who is the pawn?

SHARON. Well, in chess there are more pawns than any other piece.

KATIE. That's right. But they're also the most limited. They can only move in two directions, and other than their first move, they can only advance one square at a time.

PATRICK. They're also the least important piece.

KATIE. Yeah. *(Pause)* Unless one makes it to the other side of the board. Then they're really valuable.

ARLENE. Why?

KATIE. Cause then you can trade that pawn for one of the men your opponent has taken from you or it can become any piece you want it to.

ARLENE. Any piece?

KATIE. Any piece.

ARLENE. I'm lost. Does this relate to the Will in any way or make sense to anyone who plays chess?

PATRICK. Not me.

DOUGLAS. Not me.

KATIE. Me neither.

SHARON. I give up.

DOUGLAS. Why don't we all give up?

SHARON. No. We're going to figure this out.

KATIE. Who is the pawn?

PATRICK. Probably me. He liked me the least of all.

ARLENE. Patrick, that's not true.

DOUGLAS. You're damned right that's not true. He hated me more than all of you put together.

ARLENE. What about me? I divorced him and moved out to California.

KATIE. You're missing the point. Pawns aren't hated or even disliked. They're just considered to be the least important. But who would that be among us?

(Pause. Then **EVERYBODY** *looks at Colleen.)*

COLLEEN. Oh, thanks a lot.

SHARON. No offense, Colleen, but you *are* the maid.

KATIE. That's not fair. Colleen is a very important part of this family. You'll never know what a help she's been – especially to Dad. Not only does she keep the house clean and cook all the meals, but she was great company for Dad. The two of them ganged up on me quite a few times. She really helped make his last years here a lot of fun. And she's been a great friend to me. Her loyalty is priceless.

COLLEEN. Stop. I can't take this. *(Looks at* **SHANNON** *and runs out of the room, stage left)*

SHARON. I guess they were closer than I thought.

ARLENE. You're just figuring that out?

KATIE. They were very close. I'm going to go find her. *(Exits stage left)*

PATRICK. *(To* **ARLENE***)* So?

ARLENE. So?

PATRICK. I'd say the séance is over.

SHARON. I guess so.

DOUGLAS. Good.

> *(***DOUGLAS*** gets up and turns on the lights.)*

> *(***SHARON*** brings the candle back to Shannon's table. Looks at ***SHANNON*** and does a double take. Looks at him curiously for a few seconds, then walks away)*

PATRICK. So. *(Pause. Picks up a kaleidoscope on the table)* Do you think Colleen would miss this kaleidoscope?

ARLENE. Patrick! Put that down!

PATRICK. Hey, come on. All she did was push a broom and cook a little and she got everything. It's not fair.

ARLENE. Apparently, that's not all she did. *(Pause)* Hide it in the bedroom under your coat.

> *(***PATRICK*** hides the kaleidoscope under his sweater and exits stage left. ***ARLENE*** looks around the room and stops as she spots an empty vase on a table.)*

SHARON. He got that for you for your 10th anniversary, didn't he?

ARLENE. Yep. *(Picks up the vase and exits stage left)*

> *(***DOUGLAS*** takes the rifle off the wall and begins looking at it.)*

DOUGLAS. I've always liked this rifle.

(**ARLENE** *returns as* **DOUGLAS** *begins examining the rifle. He looks in the barrel.*

DOUGLAS. I don't believe it. The damn thing's loaded! What kind of idiot leaves a loaded rifle on the wall?

ARLENE. *(Pointing to* **SHANNON***)* That kind of idiot. For years I tried to get him to take that thing down. I think having it up there made him feel macho.

(**SHARON** *enters.* **DOUGLAS** *points the rifle at a portrait of Shannon hanging on the wall.)*

ARLENE. Douglas, be careful with that thing. It could go off.

DOUGLAS. Yeah. *(Points it at the portrait again and pretends to shoot.)*

SHARON. No! Not that. I like that painting.

DOUGLAS. Then you better get it out of here.

(**SHARON** *takes the painting off the wall and exits stage left.)*

ARLENE. He used to say that rifle made him feel safe.

DOUGLAS. *(Putting the rifle up to Shannon's head)* How does it make you feel now, old man?

ARLENE. Douglas, put that away!

DOUGLAS. Relax.

(**PATRICK** *enters.)*

PATRICK. Hey, let me see that thing.

ARLENE. No, Patrick. That's not a toy. It's a loaded rifle. You could shoot somebody.

(**DOUGLAS** *hands the rifle to Patrick.)*

DOUGLAS. For God's sake, Arlene, he's not a little kid.

PATRICK. Yeah, Mom. Take it easy. If there was going to be an accident in the house, it would have happened yesterday.

ARLENE. What do you mean?

PATRICK. Come on, Mom. Don't deny it. Just last night we were thinking up all kinds of fatal accidents that could happen.

ARLENE. We were just talking.

DOUGLAS. And hoping.

ARLENE. Well, that's in the past, and we don't have to worry about it any more.

PATRICK. *(Looking at* SHANNON*)* I have an interesting question. *(Pointing the rifle at* SHANNON*)* You can't kill someone who's already dead, right?

DOUGLAS. That's right, college boy.

PATRICK. So if you shoot somebody who's already dead, you can't get into any trouble, right?

ARLENE. Patrick, you wouldn't dare.

PATRICK. Why not?

ARLENE. The girls would have a fit. And Colleen would be madder than hell. She just cleaned in here.

DOUGLAS. Well, I'm not walking out of here empty handed. *(Takes the rifle from* PATRICK *and exits)*

PATRICK. *(Calls out)* Sharon! *(Pause)* Hey, Sharon, get your psychic-ass in here!

*(*SHARON *enters.)*

PATRICK. Didn't you want a new TV?

SHARON. Yeah, sure.

PATRICK. We'll stash it in your closet for now.

SHARON. Perfect. That's where the painting is.

PATRICK. Do you know where he hides the keys to the Ferrari?

SHARON. Yep.

*(*PATRICK *cheers as he and* SHARON *exit carrying the TV.* ARLENE *and* DOUGLAS *enter and simultaneously kneel down at opposite ends of a Persian rug and begin rolling it up.)*

ARLENE. What are you doing?

DOUGLAS. This is mine.

ARLENE. I don't think so.

DOUGLAS. Arlene, I want this rug.

ARLENE. No way.

DOUGLAS. You got the vase.

ARLENE. That vase was mine. I should have taken it with me when I moved out.

DOUGLAS. Give it up, Arlene.

ARLENE. No! I want this rug.

(DOUGLAS *pulls the rug away from* ARLENE *and they start wrestling for it.* SHARON *enters.*)

SHARON. What is going on here?

(ARLENE *and* DOUGLAS *are still holding onto opposite ends of the rug.*)

ARLENE. I want this rug!

DOUGLAS. You can't have it. Besides, it'll look better in my house.

ARLENE. How do you know? You've never even seen my house.

DOUGLAS. I don't have to. It doesn't matter what it looks like. The rug goes better with mine.

ARLENE. Does not.

DOUGLAS. Does so.

ARLENE. Does not.

DOUGLAS. Does so.

SHARON. Stop it! Listen to yourselves! You sound like a couple of two year olds.

ARLENE. He started it.

DOUGLAS. Did not.

(PATRICK *enters.*)

SHARON. I don't believe this. Look, there must be a civilized way to settle this. *(To* ARLENE*)* What color is the carpet in your living room?

(KATIE *and* COLLEEN *enter and look around the room.*)

KATIE. Are we having a garage sale?

COLLEEN. What's going on?

ARLENE. I'm sorry, Katie, but this isn't right. I gave too

much of my life to this family to end up with nothing to show for it.

KATIE. That's a lovely thing to say to your child.

ARLENE. I didn't mean it like that. You know I love you.

KATIE. I don't know what I know any more.

DOUGLAS. You probably think we're a bunch of greedy pigs, but that's too bad. I just want what I've earned.

ARLENE. You? I spent 20 years with that man.

DOUGLAS. I've been his brother all my life. That's a lot more than 20 years.

SHARON. Let's not start fighting again, okay?

ARLENE. Sorry.

COLLEEN. Where's the television?

SHARON. There's one in Dad's room and one in the den. Isn't two enough?

KATIE. What happened to the kaleidoscope?

PATRICK. How often is Colleen going to look at that?

KATIE. Dad was right. You are a pack of thieves.

PATRICK. Well, we can't all be perfect like you, now can we?

KATIE. Why don't you all just leave us alone for a while. Would you go into the den and let us have a few minutes alone with Dad?

DOUGLAS. What for?

KATIE. In case you've forgotten, this is a wake. No matter what you think of me or Colleen or Dad and his Will, this is a wake and you should have at least a little respect for the dead.

COLLEEN. Katie's right. After the wake is over you can say and do whatever you want, but for now, could we just have a moment of peace?

ARLENE. All right. We'll be in the den.

(**ARLENE, PATRICK, DOUGLAS** *and* **SHARON** *exit.* **KATIE** *walks over to* **SHANNON** *and picks up his drink.)*

KATIE. You don't mind if I have some of this, do you, Dad? You know, you could have actually pulled this off. You were very good – never moved a muscle. Never even saw you breathing. If I hadn't already known, I would have been just as sucked in by your performance as everyone else was. That's right, Dad. I know. I've known all along.

(**SHANNON** *turns his head to look at* **KATIE.**)

KATIE. Don't move. Don't even think about moving.

COLLEEN. I'm sorry, Shannon. I couldn't keep this from Katie.

KATIE. That's right. I've known from the very beginning. Not only are you not dead, you're not even sick, at least not physically. You've been plotting this for the last two years. Quite a show you put on. And all because of your sacred money. That's what this was all about – money. Well, you're right. That is what it's all about. In fact, that's the only reason I went along with this abomination. After all I've done for you in the last two years, playing along with this little charade was the only way I could make sure I got my reward. And you're going to help me with that right now. I want the combination to the safe.

(**SHANNON** *looks at* **KATIE.**)

KATIE. You didn't think I knew about that, did you, Dad? Yes, your hidden treasure has been discovered.

COLLEEN. Actually, I'm the one who discovered it. Being anal-retentive has its advantages. I found it one day when I moved the trunk to dust the baseboards.

KATIE. (*Leaning towards* **SHANNON**) Now, as quietly as possible, whisper the combination to me.

(**PATRICK** *enters.*)

PATRICK. Where did I leave my drink? (*Sees* **KATIE** *leaning close to* **SHANNON**) Oh God, what are you doing?

KATIE. Go away, Patrick!

PATRICK. That's really weird, Katie. I don't know what

you're doing, but it looks really weird.

KATIE. Get out of here!

PATRICK. Gladly! *(Exits)*

> *(COLLEEN stands at the living room entrance as if to guard it.)*

KATIE. *(Leaning towards SHANNON again)* The combination?

SHANNON. *(Whispers)* Twenty-five right, three left, fourteen right.

> *(KATIE lifts up the rug by the trunk and opens the floor safe.)*

KATIE. God damn it! *(To SHANNON)* What did you do with the money?

> *(SHANNON smiles. DR. GOLDBERG enters.)*

DR. GOLDBERG. What's taking you so long?

KATIE. Would you go back to the garage! What if somebody sees you?

> *(SHANNON looks at DR. GOLDBERG inquisitively.)*

COLLEEN. If you blow this thing, I swear I'll turn you in for fraud! Go back to the garage with your little hired helpers and finish loading the truck.

DR. GOLDBERG. I'm sorry, Shannon. If I didn't go along with this, they were going to report me to the AMA for signing a phony death certificate.

> *(SHANNON looks at DR. GOLDBERG sadly.)*

DR. GOLDBERG. I can't lose my license.

KATIE. Let's just get out of here.

> *(SHANNON, looks very distressed, then goes back into his "dead" pose.)*

DR. GOLDBERG. The U-Haul is packed and ready to go. But won't they hear the Ferrari start up?

COLLEEN. The Ferrari?

KATIE. You hooked a U-Haul up to a Ferrari?

DR. GOLDBERG. What? You'd rather take the hatchback?

KATIE. Let's just get out of here!

(KATIE, COLLEEN, *and* DR. GOLDBERG *exit.* PATRICK *and* ARLENE *enter.*)

PATRICK. Hey, where'd they go? I'm telling you, man, it was really weird. She was right in his face. It looked like she was going to kiss him or something.

ARLENE. I think we should all just call it a night. This whole thing has been an emotional strain on everybody.

PATRICK. You can go to bed if you want to, but I'm not tired.

ARLENE. All right. I'll see you in the morning. (*Kisses* PAT-RICK *and exits*)

(PATRICK *fixes himself a drink.* SHARON *and* DOUG-LAS *enter.*)

PATRICK. Mom just went to bed.

DOUGLAS. Good. She was driving me nuts. I'm so sick of hearing about her precious California.

ARLENE. (*Shouts from off stage*) Oh my God! We've been robbed! (*Enters the living room.*)

PATRICK. Robbed?

ARLENE. The bedroom – it's practically empty! (*Exits and shouts*) Katie's and Colleen's rooms are completely bare! (*Pause – then shouts*) Katie? Colleen? (*Enters the living room*)

DOUGLAS. Where are those two?

SHARON. I don't know. They were here a minute ago.

PATRICK. Yeah, and what were they doing all that time they were gone after the séance?

DOUGLAS. What the hell is going on here?

ARLENE. They've taken everything.

SHARON. What about the stuff we stashed in the closets?

ARLENE. Gone.

SHARON. Damn them!

PATRICK. At least the Ferrari's still here.

(*A loud car engine is heard*)

PATRICK. (*Screams*) No!

(**PATRICK, ARLENE,** *and* **SHARON** *exit running as the car is heard driving away.*)

DOUGLAS. *(From off stage)* A U-Haul?

PATRICK. They hooked a U-Haul up to a Ferrari?

SHARON. Let's get them!

(A car is heard starting up and screeching away. Silence. **SHANNON** *sits for about 30 seconds. Then he turns and looks towards the door. He hears a noise and returns to his "dead" pose. After about three seconds, he looks at the door again. Very slowly, he starts to move. He looks around the room. Looks at the Christmas tree.)*

SHANNON. *(Yells to the door)* Hey, you forgot the tree!

(**SHANNON** *picks up his drink and gets up. He looks around the room. He finishes his drink and puts the glass back on the table. He walks downstage and looks at the audience.)*

SHANNON. I heard about a lady who left all her money to her cat when she died. I like a girl with a sense of humor. Now that I know how well this bunch will handle it when the time comes, *(Pause)* I think I'm going to go get a cat.

End of Play

PROPERTIES

<u>ACT I</u>

Christmas Decorations
Rifle on Wall
Banner Saying "Piece on Earth"
Book for Shannon to Read
Glasses and Liquor for Bar
Decorated Christmas Tree
Six Bags of Luggage
Shannon's Glasses
Plate of Cheese and Crackers
Dishes for Dining Room Table
Wheelchair
Tray of Meat for Dinner
Desk
Pad of Paper
Pen
Business Card (Flowers)

<u>ACT II</u>

Flowers
Candles
Table
Food for Table
Ten Bottles of Irish Whiskey
Small Table
Black Table Cloth
Two White Candles
Sofa
Two Chairs
Rosary
Pair of Boots
The Will
Separate Piece of Paper for Douglas
Small Spray Bottle
Purse for Sharon
Book of Matches
Broom
Dust Pan
Rag
Kaleidoscope
Vase
Portrait of Shannon
Television
Persian Rug
Trunk

Also by **Kitty Burns...**

Identity Crisis

On Hold at 30,000 Feet

Psycho Night at the Paradise Lounge

Terminal Terror

Please visit our website **samuelfrench.com** for complete
descriptions and licensing information